Teach Your Children Well

Fables, Stories and Rhymes
for Today's World

LAURI KENT

ILLUSTRATED BY Kate Kreker

*…if your heart is wise —
then my heart will be glad indeed…*
~Proverbs 23:15

Copyright © 2023 Lauri Kent.

All rights reserved. No part of this book may be used or reproduced by any means, graphic, electronic, or mechanical, including photocopying, recording, taping or by any information storage retrieval system without the written permission of the author except in the case of brief quotations embodied in critical articles and reviews.

LifeRich Publishing is a registered trademark of The Reader's Digest Association, Inc.

LifeRich Publishing books may be ordered through booksellers or by contacting:

LifeRich Publishing
1663 Liberty Drive
Bloomington, IN 47403
www.liferichpublishing.com
844-686-9607

Because of the dynamic nature of the Internet, any web addresses or links contained in this book may have changed since publication and may no longer be valid. The views expressed in this work are solely those of the author and do not necessarily reflect the views of the publisher, and the publisher hereby disclaims any responsibility for them.

Additional Illustrations provided by:

Sea Turtle and Starfish by everysunsun
Golden Pheasant by Viktoria.1703
Papel Picado by Graphic Blue Bird

Any people depicted in stock imagery provided by Getty Images are models,
and such images are being used for illustrative purposes only.
Certain stock imagery © Getty Images.

Scriptures taken from the Holy Bible, New International Version®, NIV®. Copyright © 1973, 1978, 1984, 2011 by Biblica, Inc.™ Used by permission of Zondervan. All rights reserved worldwide. www.zondervan.com The "NIV" and "New International Version" are trademarks registered in the United States Patent and Trademark Office by Biblica, Inc.™

ISBN: 978-1-4897-4890-4 (sc)
ISBN: 978-1-4897-4891-1 (hc)
ISBN: 978-1-4897-4889-8 (e)

Library of Congress Control Number: 2023915309

Print information available on the last page.

LifeRich Publishing rev. date: 08/24/2023

The Wise Elephant

It was early evening by the great river which looped through the beautiful African wilderness. Animals, large and small, gathered along the river to drink water from the dwindling river. It was the height of the dry season and the sneaky plan of Hyena was working!

Each evening, Hyena paced along the river as the timid antelope, Takondwa, and her herd left the bush and came for their evening drink of fresh water.

Tonight, hoping to spread unhappiness, Hyena called out in a gruff voice, "Takondwa, is it fair you must share the river with others? The river shrinks day after day and the hippos leave little room for you and your herd to drink."

Timid Takondwa did not speak to sly Hyena, but her eyes narrowed as she watched the hippos gathered in the center of the shrinking river. Her face showed her anger as she glared at the hippos, as if they were intruders.

In the middle of the river, Tadala, the hippo, overheard Hyena's remarks and was insulted by them. Hoping to take advantage of the restlessness at the waterhole, Hyena called out to Tadala, "How much does one hippo drink compared to a herd of thirsty antelope?" Tadala felt *his* temper rising and he floated closer to the antelope gathered on the bank of the river.

Suddenly, a low rumbling echoed across the river and its banks. It announced the arrival of the wise, elder elephant, Adaeze, and her tight-knit family of elephants. All the animals stood quietly waiting for Adaeze to speak.

First, the wise elephant spoke to the timid antelope, "What is the meaning of your name, sweet Takondwa?"

"My name means, We are Glad," said Takondwa.

"And you, lucky Tadala, what is the meaning of your name?" Adaeze asked the hippo.

"My name means, 'We have been Blessed,'" Tadala's deep voice rumbled.

The animals stood nodding their heads while thinking about the questions from the wise Adaeze.

"And in a few short weeks, does the spring rain bring lush green life back to our valley to bless us as we raise our families?" asked Adaeze.

The animals' faces brightened at the thought of the cool rains and the wonderful green landscape that would appear in a few short weeks. Hyena saw that his weeks of spreading unhappiness in the hearts and minds of the animals beside the river was no longer working and he slinked away unnoticed.

Wise Adaeze and her herd trumpeted in delight as peace settled in across the banks of the river. And the animals, big and small, happily shared the river's gift of fresh water together.

❧

Walk with the wise and become wise ...
~ Proverbs 13:20

The Rhinoceros and Little Tick Bird

One hot day on the African grasslands, a rhinoceros was resting from the day's heat under a tree. He was half asleep when he felt a small creature land on his immense back. Snorting with impatience he called out to the intruder, "Who goes there?"

Knowing that a rhinoceros has poor eyesight and a short temper, a little bird quickly landed on a nearby bush. "It is only I, who has come as a friend," said the bright-eyed bird.

Lazily cocking just one ear toward the little bird, the rhinoceros chuckled deep in his wide chest. "Have you noticed my legs that are the size of trees and my large horns? Why is it you annoy me in this afternoon heat?"

Again, the little bird said cheerfully, "I have come as a friend. I can help keep your skin clean of insects and, in return, I only need a few hairs to line my new nest."

Grumbling, the rhinoceros turned his back on the bird and went back to dreaming about the cool mud bath he would soon be taking down by the river bed. With her feelings hurt, the little bird flew off into a nearby tree.

Suddenly, a loud screeching from above woke the rhinoceros, "Poachers, poachers straight ahead!" shrieked the voice.

In an instant, the startled rhinoceros angerly charged forward – his massive head with horns searching for his attackers. He quickly smashed the poachers plan and they ran off in every direction trying to escape his anger.

As the dust settled, the rhinoceros trotted back to the shade of the tree and called out, "Whose voice saved my life and great horns from the poachers? To you, I am forever grateful."

The little bird landed on a nearby bush and said, "I called out the danger as you slept."

From that day forward the little bright-eyed bird was seen riding piggyback on the rhinoceros' immense back as the two friends traveled across the African grasslands.

Do to others as you would have them do to you.
~Luke 6:31

The Words I Say

Guide me in the words I say
as I follow God each day.

Keep my words truthful and kind,
even when my anger blinds.

Keep my words wholesome and clean
even though I could be mean.

Keep my words of honest nature
even though lying might seem safer.

Guide me in the words I say
as I follow God each day.

☙

*Let your conversations be
always full of grace…
~Colossians 4:6*

A Gentle Answer

There once were two friends
who disagreed on a point.

One friend thought this
and one friend thought that.

After a long conversation,
nothing had changed.

So instead, they agreed they were different
which calmed the exchange.

A gentle answer turns away wrath…
~Proverbs 15:1

Young Squirrel and Young Blue Jay

Once upon a time, Young Squirrel lived with his Grandmother in the forest. One of his favorite treats were the ripe blueberries he plucked from the bushes at the edge of the forest. One day, he spotted someone new walking around his favorite bush, Young Blue Jay.

They quickly fell into a conversation and promised to meet again the next afternoon. Sunlight was fading, so Young Squirrel hurried home to avoid the keen nighttime eyesight of Owl.

At home in his cozy bed, Young Squirrel shared his new friendship with his Grandmother. "Be careful Young Squirrel," she warned, "It takes some time to discover someone's true character. It will save you great heartache in the future." Young Squirrel fell asleep wondering how to discover a friend's true character.

Early the next morning, Young Squirrel was hard at work gathering acorns for his Grandmother's breakfast when Young Blue Jay suddenly appeared.

"I found a new blueberry bush filled with ripe berries. Let's hurry and have a fine breakfast together," said Young Blue Jay.

"First I must deliver these tasty acorns to Grandmother for her early morning meal," said Young Squirrel.

"Grandmother Squirrel won't mind if you delay your delivery for a few hours," suggested Young Blue Jay.

Young Squirrel imagined the sweet taste of his favorite treat in a bush only a short journey away. Ignoring the sharp tug of his conscience, he dropped the acorns and followed Young Blue Jay, who chuckled with delight.

The day passed with great speed and the night star was sparkling in the sky as Young Squirrel crept past his sleeping Grandmother and crawled into his cold bed.

Young Blue Jay's stories of being a trickster to others in the forest were entertaining, at first. Young Blue Jay would shriek with laughter at each story as he described the sad misfortunes of others he had fooled. But each story added to the knot of unhappiness growing inside of Young Squirrel. After a long time, he finally fell into a troubled sleep.

Grandmother Squirrel woke up to a delightful surprise. Young Squirrel was sitting at her bedside with an overflowing basket of her favorite nuts. But his dark eyes were missing their normal sparkle.

"What is wrong, my sweet grandson?" asked Grandmother.

"Yesterday was not at all right," sighed Young Squirrel, shaking his head sadly.

"Hmmm," murmured Grandmother, "What troubles you so?"

"What brings laughter to another's heart, makes my heart sad," he said.

"An unhappy combination," said Grandmother, watching Young Squirrel closely.

Just then Young Robin's voice called out to Young Squirrel from the doorway, "Are you ready to play *now?*"

Young Squirrel jumped up and kissed his Grandmother. "I promise, I won't be late tonight," he said as he hurried to meet his old friend, Young Robin.

Grandmother smiled and sat thinking of the wise choices her grandson had made to avoid his future unhappiness.

Do not be misled: Bad company corrupts good character.
~1 Corinthians 15:33

Little Sparrow and Hawk

There once was a Little Sparrow who went on a big adventure. He had recently learned to fly and today he was soaring higher than he had ever flown before!

Flutter, flutter, glide… he pushed his little wings to carry him high up into the bright blue sky. Filled with excitement, he soon found himself near the top of a tall pine tree.

Little Sparrow's tired little wings began to fail him and he landed, *thump*, beside the largest nest he had ever seen.

His tiny black eyes peered with interest at the contents of the nest. A large leaf partially filled with sparkling rainwater quickly caught his attention. As he stood beside the nest wishing for a much-needed drink of water, the sky suddenly grew dark as night. A high-pitched screech announced the arrival of the owner of the nest, Hawk.

Quickly Little Sparrow introduced himself, "My apologies to you, fine sir. I was on an adventure when my new wings grew ever so heavy and I landed quite uninvited by the side of your nest."

Now Hawk had been caught by surprise by Little Sparrow's unplanned arrival, but he quickly thought of a dishonest plan. "I will fatten him up and have him as a fine dinner," thought Hawk.

So Hawk, with a voice like honey, said, "Come inside my nest Little Sparrow, to drink and eat to your heart's content. You need not lift a feather, for I will supply you with all that you wish for or desire."

Little Sparrow hopped a small step closer, still wishing for a sip of the rainwater sparkling in a large leaf near Hawk's sharp talons.

Instead, Little Sparrow paused to listen to his head and heart, and chirped, "Thank you fine sir, I must be off to work for my own dinner." And Little Sparrow flew away quickly, leaving the company of dishonest Hawk.

The prudent see danger…
~Proverbs 27:12

Setting the Table

First set the napkins, all on the left;
The fork sits on top, just like a nest.

The tall knife settles in on the right;
Next the spoon jumps in to snuggle up tight!

Now place the plate right in the center;
Setting the table always makes dinner taste better!

Pick Up, Pack Up!

Pick up, pack up, it's time for bed;
"Yes, ma'am, Yes, sir," is what I said.

Pick up, pack up, it's time for prayers;
"Thank you, thank you for your loving care."

Do everything without complaining or arguing...
~Philippians 2:14.

Three Brothers Choose a Tree

Once upon a time, in a forest high up in a shady oak tree lived three woodpecker brothers. Their mother loved them each despite their very different personalities. Sadly, it was time for the three brothers to leave the cozy nest and use their talents in the world.

The oldest brother chose to leave first. He was the largest of the brothers. His square head with chisel-like bill matched his stubborn personality. Overflowing with confidence, he located a sturdy tree and began carving an enormous hole for his new home.

The middle brother was smaller in size than his older brother, but he boasted that his quick chiseling skills would help him carve out a fine new home. Impatient to get started, he left in a blur of black and white checkered wings.

The smallest brother was the last to leave. His thoughtful disposition had allowed him to sit and listen to the elder woodpeckers' wisdom. As he flew away, he vowed to his mother he would take his time and carve a nest hidden from Hawk's sharp vision.

The oldest brother after weeks of working, found his newly built home was too large and drafty. Blowing rain during summer storms added to his misery by soaking the entrance to his nest. But his stubborn nature convinced him to stay instead of dealing with the problem at hand.

In a tree nearby, the middle brother was having troubles of his own. He had carved out his nest in less than a week but it was barely large enough to squeeze inside. He grumbled each time he tried to turn because his long tail feathers would bunch up in the most uncomfortable way. Instead of dealing with the problem at hand, his impatient nature convinced him to rush from tree to tree, in search of tasty bark beetles.

Meanwhile, the youngest brother searched the forest for a branch to carve his new home. He hopped up and down branches tapping the tree bark for just the right sound. *Tap, tap, hop, hop, tap, tap,* for days he searched. Finally, after a week of searching, he began carving out a new nest on the underside of a dead branch, hidden from the keen eyes of Hawk.

Years passed and, from time to time, the youngest brother was able to visit with his family in the forest. His oldest brother would complain loudly that his home was too large and drafty. Grumbling, the middle brother would interrupt him to complain he wished *he* had more room to stretch out his long tail feathers.

The youngest brother just smiled and was grateful he had listened to his elders many years ago.

The wise store up knowledge…
~Proverbs 10:14

The Sheep and the Green Frog

There once was a young sheep who lived high up on the peaks of the mountains. Instead of grazing on shrubs with her winter herd, the young ewe spent most of her time gazing at herself in a small glacier lake.

Staring at her reflection, she admired her slender horns that curved ever so slightly backwards. She marveled at her delicate split hoofs which helped her leap from rock to rock on the steep cliffside she called home.

But her greatest fascination was with her beautiful tan coat. It was her greatest pride and she gazed into the lake daily to admire her own beauty.

Cascading waterfalls and rushing streams from the snowmelt announced the arrival of spring. The herd and the young Ewe moved down to the budding green plains in the lower valley. It did not take long for the young Ewe to find a ripple-free pond to again gaze at her reflection. As she stood admiring her beautiful tan coat, a green frog basking on a rock interrupted her thoughts.

"Young Ewe, why do you stand here hour upon hour," croaked Frog, "instead of seeking the tender green grass?"

The young Ewe gave an impatient snort and glared at Frog. "I am admiring my beautiful tan coat," she boasted, turning her head for a better view of her reflection.

Frog observed small clumps of the young sheep's winter coat were already shedding in the summer heat. Frog thought, "I will try and turn the young Ewe's focus to the beauty that is surrounding her."

Frog in an encouraging voice said, "Look around you, nature's beauty surrounds you in this beautiful meadow with its wonderful pond!"

But the young Ewe continued to stare at her reflection in the pond turning her head from side-to-side to admire her tan coat and slender horns. Seeing no change in the young Ewe's self-admiring gaze, Frog hopped off singing softly,

> "Little, little, does she know;
> Her tan coat will soon
> dissolve like snow."

༄

Your beauty should not come from outward adornments…
instead, it should be that of your inner self…
~1 Peter 3: 3-4

One Green Sea Turtle

One green sea turtle swam out to sea;
Laughing he shouted,
"Come and count with me!"

Two grey Humpback's swam side-by-side;
A mother and baby;
Swimming together on the morning tide.

Three red lobsters were playing a game;
Big claws clicking and clacking;
Each trying to earn a famous nickname.

Four blue-tailed triggerfish dig;
Blowing out jets of water;
And grunting like a pig.

Five black manta rays glide and turn;
With their giant mouths open;
Searching for plankton is their only concern.

Six white-bellied dolphins jumped and spun;
Dancing on the water;
Splashing just for fun.

Seven orange starfish on the ocean floor;
Feeding on clams and mussels;
Curious creatures, always looking for more.

Eight pink coral colonies brighten the sea;
Sheltering the sea animals,
With branches shaped like leaves.

Nine grey monk seals dive down deep;
To hunt on the sea floor:
What prey will they meet?

Ten yellow tang fish swim slowly by;
Count them with me.
1, 2, 3, 4, 5, 6, 7, 8, 9, 10!

One green sea turtle, filled with glee,
"Thank you for counting
Sea creatures with me!"

So God created the great creatures of the sea...
~Genesis 1:21

Golden Pheasants

Once upon a time, outside a small village high up in the mountains, a young boy lived with his mother and father on a small plot of land. Although they had very few possessions, they lived a happy life tending to their fields and flock of chickens.

As a baby, Chao, had been carried on his mother's back while she worked on the land and fed the chickens. As he grew, Chao would help his mother. Each morning, he would open the enclosure door to let the hens out to search for tasty seeds and berries. Then together, they would carefully collect the eggs placing them gently in baskets to be sold at the market by his father.

Now that Chao was older, it was his responsibility to let the chickens out in the morning and collect their eggs. And most importantly, at the end of the day, Chao would lead the chickens back to the safety of their enclosure. This protected them from the predators that roamed the mountains at night.

One evening, as the sun began to set, Chao saw his father returning from the market with a crate filled with birds with magnificent feathers of gold, blue and black. Chao ran to his father, curious to see the contents of the crate. Father set the crate down gently in the enclosure and waited for Mother to join them.

"Son," Father explained in a quiet voice, "I have purchased golden pheasants to add to our flock. Under our watchful care, their precious eggs and feathers will be sold at the market to prosper our family. For they are prized far more than the chicken eggs." Chao gazed with admiration at the shimmering crowns of the golden pheasants.

"Chao," said his father, "you must take great care of these magnificent pheasants. They are shy birds and they need calm words to keep them from taking flight into the trees to roost."

Nodding his head, Chao agreed to his important role in the family's future as he gazed admiringly at the elegant golden pheasants who were now timidly mingling with the chickens.

For weeks, Chao worked with the golden pheasants, bringing them tender bamboo shoots and berries to earn their trust. Speaking quietly, he learned to call them into the enclosure each evening to roost in safety from the nighttime predators.

Tonight was different. Chao was frustrated, he was almost late for dinner. Impatient to leave, Chao shouted, shaking his fist at the largest of the golden pheasants who would not enter the enclosure. In a sudden burst of energy, it flew off into the forest as the light faded from the sky. Chao stood with his hands by his side, in stunned silence, staring after the lost pheasant. Now what should he do? His father and mother had trusted him with the care of the golden-headed pheasants and now one had flown off into the dark forest. It would be a great loss for his family. Surely, he would be punished.

Thoughts raced through Chao's mind. Maybe he should tell his parents he only counted three during his morning chores, so surely one must have escaped during the night. Or maybe he should say one golden pheasant had never returned to the enclosure, even after he gently called them. Only neither of these stories were true.

Chao walked slowly back to the house to speak with his father and mother about the terrible loss of one of the golden pheasants. He wondered what his punishment would be.

Standing in front of them, he thought, "I need to tell the truth." So he said, "It was my fault; I was frustrated. I yelled so loudly I frightened a pheasant and he flew off into the forest."

And much to his surprise, his father sat calmly at the table and said, "Yes, tonight our family will lose a fine bird to the predators of the forest. But most importantly, our dear son, you did not fall into temptation to lie and you told us the truth. This honorable act is much more important to us."

Honor your father and mother...
~Ephesians 6:2

Sofia's Sunshine

As the sun rose, Señor Vega and his donkey walked down the middle of the narrow cobblestone street. Plodding along past the brightly colored houses, the old donkey walked clip, clop, clip, clop beside his master on their way to the market in the plaza.

Just like every other morning, Sofia from her window seat, raised her hand in greeting and smiled. And just like every other morning, Señor Vega and his donkey walked by in silence.

"Sofia, your breakfast is ready," called her mother. Sofia rushed to the kitchen, "Good morning, Mamá and Papá!" "Buenos días," they replied together. They smiled at Sofia, feeling grateful for the sunshine she brought to their lives each day.

After breakfast, each hurried off to their chores. Papá went to the market for fresh chicken and vegetables for the family restaurant. Mamá, dressed in her white dress embroidered with colorful flowers, left for the restaurant to prepare silverware for the dinner guests.

Sofia's morning chore was to pick fresh flowers from the garden for the tables at the restaurant. She moved through the garden with skilled hands, gathering colorful flowers and greens in her flower basket. When her basket was full, Sofia started the short walk to the restaurant. As she walked, she thought of an idea.

Sofia stopped at the home of Señora Flores. Simmering smells of delicious food floated out the door when the elderly Señora Flores in her white apron opened the door. "Good morning," said Sofia as she handed her some of the brightly colored flowers. "Gracias, sweet child," called out the surprised Señora Flores as she watched happy Sofia skip down the narrow street toward the restaurant.

After Sofia had arranged the flowers for the tables, she had a few hours to herself as her parents prepared the food for their nighttime dinner crowd. She stopped by the backyard of Señora Luna and her four young children. "Good morning, Señora Luna, how can I help today?" asked Sofia. A frazzled Señora Luna said, "What a blessing you are Sofia. I must run these freshly made tablecloths over to my husband at the plaza market. Could you watch the children for a few minutes?"

"Of course," said Sofia as she gathered the children around the backyard table. In a few minutes Sofia and the children were making a colorful *Papel Picado* by cutting out patterns in colored tissue paper to hang as decorations. The children laughed as they snipped the tiny patterns and Sofia hung them on a line.

Just as they finished, Señora Luna arrived back at the house. "Bravo," she said with a smile, "such a delightful surprise!" Sofia slipped out the side gate as Señora Luna and her children admired the brightly colored paper flags waving in the breeze.

Sofia still had time before lunch and siesta, so she walked over to see if Señor Cano was in his special chair in front of his son's music store. "Good morning, Señor Cano, can I read for you today?" Señor Cano's elderly eyes strained at the fine print in his open Bible. "Yes, what a blessing you are, sweet Sofia." Sofia settled at Señor Cano's feet and began reading his favorite passage as the sun rose high in the sky. From inside the store, Señor Cano's son looked up and saw the pair on the porch as he sat and strummed a six-string guitar for a customer.

The rest of the day and night raced by. Later, as Sofia's family sat by the outside fire, Papá shared the stories told at the restaurant that evening. Señora Flores had cooked a fine dinner for Señor Vega and had stopped by his booth at the plaza market to deliver it. She even brought an apple for his donkey. It was the first time anyone had seen Señor Vega smile in years!

Señora Luna and her children had stretched out the colorful *Papel Picado* across the street in front of the shops. The colorful flags inspired Señor Cano and his son to bring out their instruments and play music in the front of the shop for hours as the children and adults danced in the moonlight.

Sofia smiled as she listened to her parents' happy voices. And as she fell asleep leaning against her Mamá, she wondered if Señor Vega would wave to her tomorrow morning.

...let your light shine before others...
~Matthew 5:16

Things I Do

Guide me in the things I do;
Keep my actions kind and true.

Keep me helpful in my chores;
knowing deeds of mine can open doors.

Keep me kind and helpful to others;
for we are designed to love one another.

Keep me determined to be wise;
let me accept instruction as a prize,

Guide me in the things I do;
Keep my actions kind and true.

Pay attention and listen to the sayings of the wise…
~Proverbs 22:17

Printed in the USA
CPSIA information can be obtained
at www.ICGtesting.com
LVHW060456021023
759825LV00012B/248